The Fifth and Final Sun

AN ANCIENT AZTEC MYTH OF THE SUN'S ORIGIN

RETOLD AND ILLUSTRATED BY C. SHANA GREGER

HOUGHTON MIFFLIN COMPANY   BOSTON   1994

To my brother Roger

Copyright © 1994 by C. Shana Greger

All rights reserved. For information about permission to reproduce selections from this book, write to Permissions, Houghton Mifflin Company, 215 Park Avenue South, New York, New York 10003.

Library of Congress Cataloging-in-Publication Data

Greger, C. Shana (Carol Shana)
   The fifth and final sun / written and illustrated by C. Shana Greger.
      p.   cm.
   Summary: For hundreds and hundreds of years different gods take turns being the sun, with unsatisfactory results, until Nanautzin takes the position permanently.
   ISBN 0-395-67438-7
   1. Aztecs — Legends.   2. Aztecs — Religion and mythology — Juvenile literature.   (1. Sun — Folklore.   2. Aztecs — Legends.   3. Indians of Mexico — Legends.)   I. Title.
F1219.76.F65G74 1994   93-11159
398.2'0972 — dc20   CIP
                              AC

Printed in the United States of America

BP   10   9   8   7   6   5   4   3   2   1

Author's Note

The Aztecs', or Nahuas', first attempts to understand the universe took the form of a great body of myths. These stories vary; the sun creation myth appears in more than ten chronicles and annals. The basic structure of *The Fifth and Final Sun* is taken from a sixteenth-century Nahua manuscript, "Leyenda de los Soles," or "Legend of the Suns," which corresponds closely with the story as recorded in hieroglyph on the ancient Aztec Calendar Stone, a pre-Hispanic monument.

The details of the creation of the fifth sun were taken from writings by Sahagún, and the early appearance of the giants and the Evening Star and the lifting of the earth and sky come from other versions of the sun myth. The survival of the giant race after the fall of the first sun, the role of the Evening Star, and Chalchihuitlicue's shortened reign are my own additions.

Research into the depictions and changing forms of the gods inspired dialogue and provided additional information for their portrayals in the illustrations. The illustration borders are based on Aztec patterns and are related generally to the main characters or the action of the picture they frame. The design of the initial capital letters is based on their corresponding symbols from the Calendar Stone, which marks the day on which a particular age ended and was named.

The First Sun

here was a time when there was no sun. Back when the world began, the White Evening Star God shone all alone in the dark sky.

In this long-ago time, there were no people on the Earth, only giants. They had huge eyes to help them see in the faint starlight. They also had huge hands and feet, though no one knows why.

For ages the Evening Star struggled to light the Earth. Still, Tezcatlipoca, the God of the Night, was stronger. "Oh, Evening Star," whispered Tezcatlipoca. "Why do you try so hard? Can't you see that your little light hardly makes a difference?"

The Evening Star shuddered, and the God of the Night began to laugh. With that, the Evening Star called on all her strength. In one great burst of energy, she lit the sky for a second, then fell.

Alone in the darkness, Tezcatlipoca turned himself into a large star, the First Sun. And the sky was evenly lit, though dimly, by the First Sun for 676 years.

The Second Sun

t so happened that Quetzalcoatl, who looked like the jade-colored quetzal bird and who was the God of the Wind, was jealous of Tezcatlipoca and became angry.

"It doesn't seem right that the day should be ruled by the God of the Night," Quetzalcoatl thought every day for 676 years, and his anger grew within him until he could be still no longer.

He howled at the First Sun, "Tezcatlipoca, God of the Night, I challenge you to a duel!"

"I accept your challenge, God of the Wind," replied the First Sun. "I know that I am much stronger than you."

Quetzalcoatl knew this was true, and he began to plot. That very evening, in the darkest part of the night, the God of the Wind took a heavy club, crept close, and with one fierce blow knocked the Sun into the ocean.

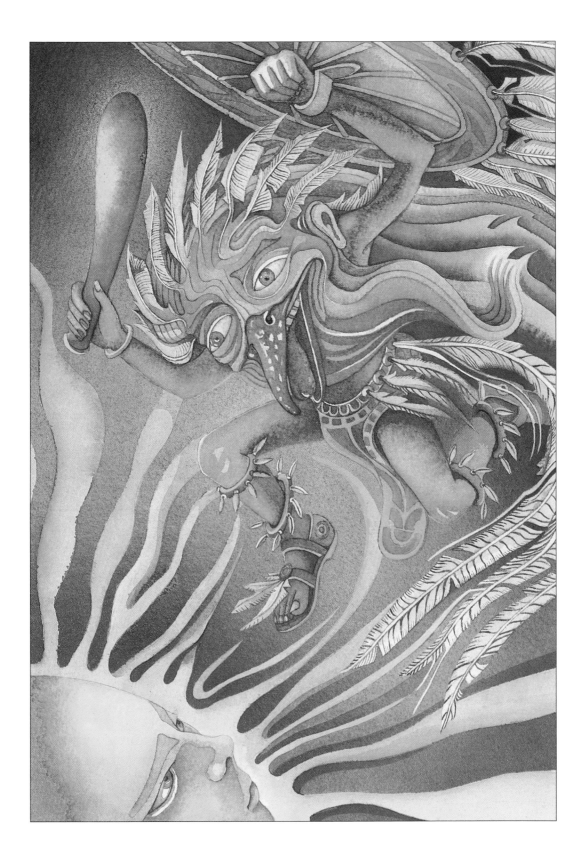

The First Sun almost drowned, but being God of the Night he turned himself into a tiger. The long swim to the shore made the tiger so hungry that when he got there he devoured all but a few of the giants.

Then, being full as well as tired, the God of the Night forgot to change his shape when he returned to the sky, and the spots on his coat shone as stars in the darkness. And there he rested.

The Earth was once again blanketed in a dreary dimness, lit only by the spots on Tezcatlipoca's fur and the Evening Star, who had climbed back into the sky.

After a while, Quetzalcoatl took over as the Second Sun and lit the sky for 364 years. The Second Sun shone a bit more brightly than the first; the world became a tiny bit warmer, and the grass grew just a few inches taller. Little by little, the giants returned.

The Third Sun

y the time 364 years had passed, the God of the Night had, in his turn, become jealous. Although by night he ruled the sky, by day the spots on his coat were completely invisible. One day at noon, when he was most angry, he reached out his great tiger claw, snatched up the Second Sun, and threw him several hundred miles across the sky.

"How dare you shine more brightly than I," he roared.

The Second Sun, taken completely by surprise, was speechless—except for his howling, which bounced off the mountains and echoed for days.

As the Second Sun rolled and tumbled across the sky, a great hurricane rose and carried everything away: all of the giants' herds and houses, even the trees, were torn from their roots. The storm had magical powers as well and changed the giants into monkeys. Finally the God of the Wind splashed into the ocean.

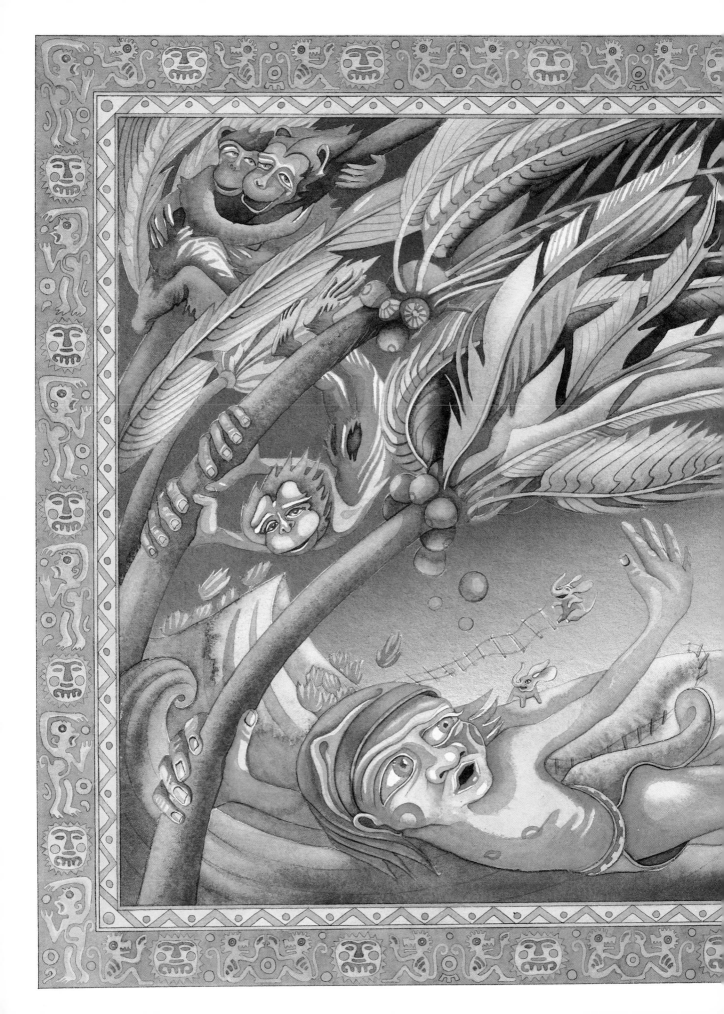

So mightily did the fall of the Second Sun shake the Earth that even the God of the Underworld was startled. Many other Gods protested. Angered and exhausted with the fighting, they declared, "Neither the God of the Wind nor the God of the Night shall ever be allowed to become Sun again."

Then they chose Tlalloc, the God of Rain, Thunder, and Lightning to become the Third Sun, even though his powers were minor compared to those of the God of the Wind or the God of the Night.

During the reign of the Third Sun, the Earth returned again to the circle of day and night. Gradually, the damage from the great hurricane disappeared and the monkeys began to thrive. The weather was always pleasant, as Tlalloc was so busy being the Third Sun that he had only a little time left over for rainmaking. Tlalloc's children, the clouds, danced and played in the sky. The Third Sun brightened the days of 312 years.

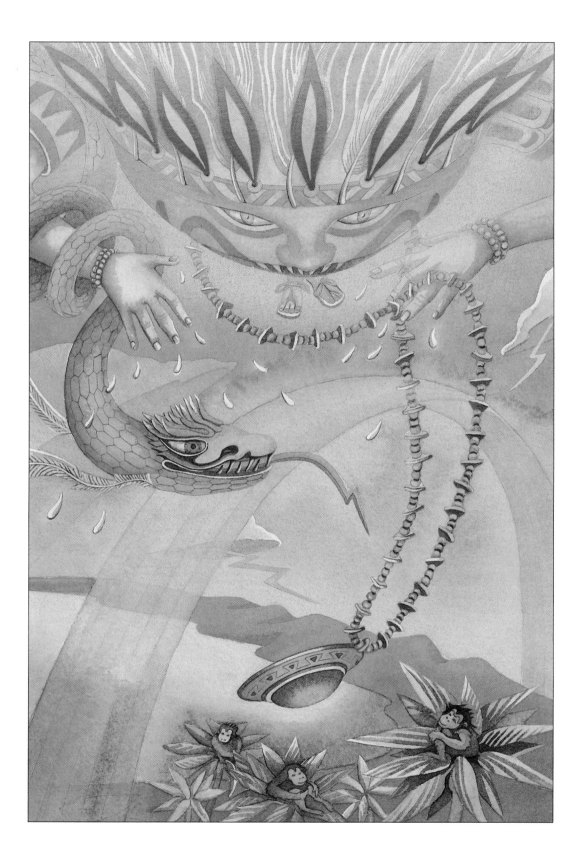

The Fourth Sun

he God of the Wind, however, was not pleased. He brooded and sulked for the whole 312 years of the Third Sun's reign until suddenly his wrath exploded. He unchained the winds and even forced them up from inside the Earth. He didn't stop until every inch of the world was covered with red-hot lava.

The Third Sun struck back but was no match for the mighty God of the Wind. He slowly slipped from the sky.

Meanwhile, most of the monkeys had perished. But not all—a few had turned themselves into turkeys and glided above the dark, steaming Earth until the lava cooled and hardened.

Then, feeling a tiny bit of shame, the God of the Wind asked Tlalloc's Wife, Chalchihuitlicue, the Goddess of the Waters, to become the Fourth Sun.

For almost 676 years, the Goddess of the Waters warmed the world in great glory. She filled the lakes and streams with crystal-clear water, and the Earth became so beautiful and green that the Gods sent two new creatures, Man and Woman, to watch over it.

Everyone was happy except the God of the Night, who
did not wish anyone to rule longer than his own 676 years.
On the evening of the next to last day of the 676th year of
the Fourth Sun's reign, the God of the Night began to
torment the Goddess of the Waters.

"What a weak and silly Sun you are. You are selfish and
unworthy. You don't really care about the Earth, you care
about being Sun only for your own glory!"

So quick were his insults that the Goddess of the Waters
had no chance to reply. She began to cry. She cried so
hard, and for so long, that the heavens fell. Almost all the
people, and even the highest mountains, were swallowed
by the floods. Only one couple survived, having hidden
in the trunk of a huge cypress tree. Most of the birds flew
away, and the turkeys—who had long since forgotten
how to fly—and all of the other creatures became fish.
Just short of 676 years lighting the Earth, the Fourth Sun
drowned in her own tears.

The Fifth Sun

fter some time of darkness had passed, the God of the Night became sorry for what he had done, even though he now ruled the sky.

He summoned the God of the Wind, and together they lifted the Earth out of the water. Then they raised the sky and rested it on top of the Rose Tree and the Tree of the Mirror.

Since the Earth was still in darkness, a meeting of all the Gods was called. As butterflies, gophers, great horned beetles, grasshoppers, and bullfrogs, they all came dancing to Teotihuacán, their sacred city. They agreed that the position of Sun would be given through a rite of sacrifice. Only in this way could they be certain that the Fifth Sun would be a permanent one.

"Who will sacrifice themselves so the Earth may have light?" asked the Gods.

Two Gods stepped forward: Tecciztecal, the proud God of the Snails, and Nanautzin, who was so ugly everyone called him the Scabby-Pimply One. He was God of something, but no one remembered what.

The sacrificial ceremony began. The two Gods fasted for four days, and on midnight of the fourth day, the Goddess of the Hearth lit the fire. So great was the blaze that mountainous shadows were cast against the high black peaks surrounding the city.

The God of the Snails stepped forward and offered rich feathers, pieces of gold, and precious jewels to the flames. But when the Gods commanded him, "Jump into the fire!" he was afraid and turned away. He tried three more times, but each time he hesitated.

So the Scabby-Pimply One came forward. He humbly offered green branches tied together, pieces of hay, and thorns covered with his own blood. Then he offered one more thing in the silence of his heart, his sincere desire to help the Earth. When the Gods commanded him, "Jump into the fire!" he took a deep breath and, rushing forward, threw himself into the very center of the blaze.

Immediately a flame shot up and headed straight through the bowl of the sky to settle in the place of high noon. So mighty a roar arose from the gathering of the Gods that the Earth shook. Everyone danced and celebrated the birth of the Fifth and Final Sun.

The Moon

t also happened that the God of the Snails, in his despair at having lost his chance to become the Sun, threw himself upon the dying flames. From the ashes, in the same part of the east, rose the Moon.

But the Gods saw that the Sun and the Moon shone with the same brightness, and they were dismayed.

"How can this be?" they said. "Is it well that they are equal?"

One of the Gods, angry, snatched up a nearby rabbit and flung it at the face of the God of the Snails. The Moon's splendor dimmed. This is also why, sometimes, you can see a rabbit on the face of the Moon when it is full.

Then the Gods noticed that the Sun was still.

"How can we live?" they said. "Let us all surround the Sun, that he may come alive through our death."

So they all died, giving their energy to the Sun. Soon the wind began to blow with a strong blast and caused the Sun to move, the moon trailing forever behind.